Minx and Spanner

Minx and Spanner

Dougie Max

illustrated by Dave Hill

Matador
Unit E2 Airfield Business Park,
Harrison Road, Market Harborough,
Leicestershire. LE16 7UL
Tel: 0116 2792299
Email: books@troubador.co.uk
Web: www.troubador.co.uk/matador
Twitter: @matadorbooks

ISBN 978 1803135 465

British Library Cataloguing in Publication Data.
A catalogue record for this book is available from the British Library.

Printed and bound by CPI Group (UK) Ltd, Croydon, CR0 4YY
Typeset in 12pt Minion Pro by Troubador Publishing Ltd, Leicester, UK

Matador is an imprint of Troubador Publishing Ltd

This book is dedicated to my grandchildren as they inspired me to put my storytelling talent into a printed book, so this book is for them.

Chapter One

"Meow."

I think this means 'hi' in your language. My name is Minx. I am an extremely white, Scottish, furry cat and I am the boss in my house.

I share the house with my human parents, a white-haired parent, a blonde-haired parent, and another pet, a chicken. Yes, I said a *chicken*!

I rule the roost in this house, and *I AM NOT* a chicken. I don't really like the chicken. It's called Myrtle.

I have my own bed, my own food station, and a state-of-the-art cat flap. The cat flap is mine alone. The chicken keeps trying to get through it, but she can't as it's extremely high-tech. You see, I have a special tartan collar that has a microchip inside it all about me with my name and address printed on the back of it. My collar opens the flap if I get near to it. Only I have the chip and only I can get through the flap.

I have the run of the house really. Only, the chicken gets in my way sometimes.

Myrtle's got a chicken coop out in the back garden, and she shares it with another five chickens. She is the only chicken that gets into the house. Apparently, she is a prize-winning chicken and has won competitions around the country. (Don't know why, I think she's ugly compared to me.) Quite often the white-haired parent brings her into the house to clean and tidy her up, spraying different stuff on her feathers and trimming her nails. I heard them saying they were getting her ready for a competition show coming up soon.

I get lots of attention too, but I get this attention every day! My parents love me. I go where I want and do what I want, and every night my parents sit and stroke me, and all I do is purrrrr! It's an easy life.

On this day, it was Myrtle's turn to get pampered, so I decided to go out for a walk. I walked towards my cat flap and, just like magic, the flap popped open.

I sometimes just walk past it to try to trick it and see if it opens, but nope, it opens every time.

Anyway, as I went out the flap, Myrtle was standing staring at some ants for some reason. I just walked past her.

Chapter Two

There are a few cats and dogs who live near us, and we all have our little area we call our territory. We don't like anyone trespassing into our territory, although we all do it.

There's an annoying sheepdog across the road called Lucky. He's a black and white sheepdog and he only has three legs due to a car accident, and only has one eye because of another accident. (*I think they should change his name.*) He barks constantly behind a six-foot fence.

There's a small opening in the fence, enough for him to stick his nose out, and quite often I'll sneak up to the opening and wait for him to stick his nose out. When he does, I scream to frighten him.

It's hilarious watching him scrambling away backwards on his two back legs, bouncing off different things in the garden. But he soon forgets and comes back and does the same thing the next day. He never learns, silly dog.

A few doors away lives a dog called Oscar. He has far too much energy! Every time I sit at the bottom of his driveway, he comes bouncing out and runs around me, round and round, falling down, doing somersaults. It's like he has springs on his feet and, wait for it… he's trying to catch his own tail! What's that all about? Dogs have no brains. He's also famous for eating strange things. Up till now he has eaten about ten remote controls, money, keys, letters, and we've lost count of how many socks.

His parents say they can't leave anything lying about or it's gone. He eats anything and everything. I wonder if they actually feed him.

Two doors along lives a ginger-haired cat called Spanner. Strange name, you're thinking... He's called that because of a mark on the fur on his back that looks just like the shape of a spanner. I quite like him. He's handsome and I know he likes me. He was sitting on his driveway when I passed him. I stopped and sat there for a while, staring at him. He never said anything, just stared back. We sat for a while in the sun looking at each other.

I was sitting grooming myself when I decided to go home. As I did, Spanner followed close behind me. I crawled under Spanner's parents' old car parked outside his house and Spanner followed me. When we came out the other side, Spanner had a black oil stripe right down the centre of his back covering the spanner-shaped mark on his fur and he had black oil marks on the tips of his ears. I also had a black oil stripe on my back and on the tips of my ears too. We both looked *sooo* different! But the same marks made us similar.

As I reached my driveway, a white van drew up outside. It was a pet food supplier. The van had big, bold, colourful pictures of cats, dogs, and chickens on its side panels. A man with a limp was delivering supplies to our house.

It looked like he had one shoe bigger than the other. I've seen him many times before; he grunted and groaned as he threw a bag of cat food onto his shoulders and stomped up the steep driveway.

The back doors of the van had been left open and some pet treats had spilled onto the road outside, which we both scoffed. I think the man with the limp had dropped them. I could hear noises coming from inside the van, like maybe other cats, or dogs. I have always been nosey and decided to jump up into the van to see what was in there. There were more treats lying on the floor of the van. I ate some and Spanner jumped in, following me. He was eating the treats too.

A moment later, the back doors slammed shut and we were suddenly in complete darkness.

I heard the back doors lock. I stood rigid. I couldn't move, and I couldn't see a thing. I heard a noise like the van's engine starting up and then moving off. Suddenly we were thrown about in the back of the van. It was moving fast and every time it braked or turned, it threw us about, bouncing off the inside panels and the back doors of the van.

Although cats' eyes are great, we could see little and after a while the van stopped. I lay in a corner exhausted. It was totally dark. I could barely see Spanner's shadow, but I knew he was there. I could hear him breathing. He was trembling like me. The last time I was in a car was to go to the vet and that was not a good experience, and for some reason I thought this journey was worse already. It all went quiet. I could still hear Spanner breathing next to me. I was scared that the light would never come back on. I could hear men's voices outside. I told Spanner to get ready, and if the door opened, we should make a run for it. He agreed.

Chapter Three

The van's alarm bleeped, and the back door locks clicked open. We could hear muffled voices in the background. Both back doors swung open, and the bright sunlight poured in. It blinded me for a moment. Two dark silhouetted figures stood in the doorway. I screamed, "RUN, Spanner, RUN."

I grabbed Spanner and we both shot out of the van's back doors, brushing past the two men and spinning them around. Both men jumped back, getting a fright as we leapt past them, shouting and screaming, "RUN, RUN, RUN!" And we did. We ran like the wind.

It was a while before we stopped. We both were exhausted and slowed down, then climbed up a tree to safety. I was so tired and out of breath I couldn't speak. We lay there clinging on to the tree, panting. I was holding on to Spanner, not knowing what to do next. We looked all around us. The surroundings were strange.

We both looked as far as our eyes could see. There were miles and miles of trees and grass. Once we calmed down, we looked back in the direction we'd come from, and we saw a huge barn and a farmhouse. By this time, we knew we were lost and far from home. I noticed my tartan collar was missing! It was my only link to my family and home, and it was gone. I probably lost it in the van or when I was running to escape the two men. I was thinking we would never get back home now.

Meanwhile… back at home, my white-haired parent was going crazy. Both myself and Spanner were missing, and all the neighbours were out looking for us. My white-haired parent called the vet to see if they could check the tracking device fitted into my collar. The call went straight to the answering machine telling them that they were closed and to leave a message, and if it was urgent, someone would get back to them. He left a message and both parents waited for the vet to call back.

Chapter Four

Meanwhile... we were still up the tree.

It was getting dark, and we were so scared. Spanner said we should go back to the barn. I agreed and we made our way slowly back there, hoping we could shelter there for the night. As we made our way back to the barn, we saw a small hole in the side of the barn and sneaked in through it for shelter. As we went through, we could not believe our eyes. It was dark, but we could see and hear other cats and dogs in cages.

Some were chained up. None of them looked great. There was a really bad smell in the air too. We decided to crawl into a corner and wait till morning.

It was very cold. The wind was howling through the gaps in the wooden barn walls. We snuggled together to keep each other warm and tried to sleep. As it got lighter, the sunlight shone through the cracks in the wooden door, slowly lighting up different areas of the barn like a searchlight. Some of the sun beams shone into the cages. We could see some sad-looking cats and dogs chained up inside their cages.

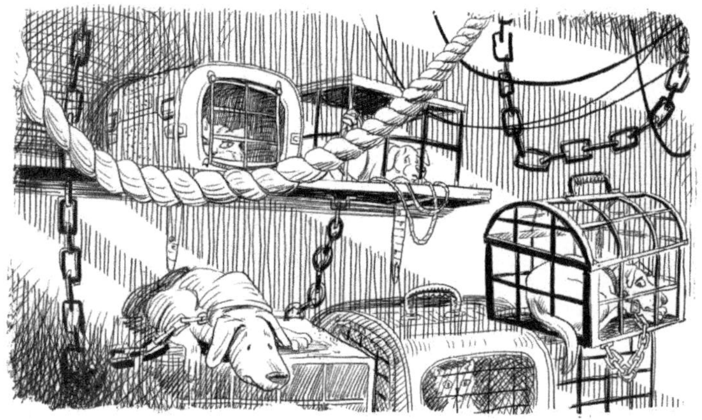

Later that morning, we could see and speak to the other cats and dogs who were caged. It turns out that the two men lured cats and dogs into their van with treats and captured them to sell them on to other people in different areas. We were alerted that the same two guys were coming into the barn.

They immediately noticed us and grabbed the both of us. They threw us into two separate cages. We were next to each other and very scared.

With the doors wide open, the sunlight poured in and we could see all around us now. There were many more cats and dogs in separate cages. None of them looked well. As the two men were leaving the barn, the man with the limp grabbed Spanner's cage, and the other man grabbed mine. Spanner looked terrified, and so was I.

The men took us into the farmhouse. They banged both our cages onto a huge wooden table. I heard one of the men on the phone saying, "Your cat is ready for collection." He grabbed Spanner from his cage by the scruff of his neck. Spanner was trying to fight him off, but the man was too big and strong. Spanner still had the oil stripe on his back and ears; he looked a mess. The man with the limp prised the lid off a large tin can and picked a collar from it. It looked like my tartan collar! It was my collar, and he strapped my collar on Spanner's neck, then threw him back into the cage.

Soon after that there was a loud knock on the door. The man with the limp opened it.

I could see a family standing on their doorstep. The kids rushed in; they were jumping up and down, super excited. They were here to pick up their new cat. I couldn't believe it when the man pointed to Spanner's cage. They all gathered round him. Spanner was jumping about the cage scared, not knowing what was happening. The kids were so excited to see him, they were shouting out different names to call him. I saw the man with the limp taking money from the kids' father and then they left. I was screaming, "Spanner, don't go." He looked so scared as he stared back at me. I shouted, "I'll find you! I'll come after you."

BANG… The farmhouse door slammed shut. Spanner was gone. I cried… I was all alone now.

Chapter Five

Meanwhile… back home.

The vet had called my parents back and told them the tracking device wasn't working for some reason. After an hour or so they contacted them again saying they had picked up a signal. It must have been when they took my collar out of the tin and put it around Spanner's neck, just before leaving the farmhouse. The signal was moving fast and probably in a car. The vet said they would keep them informed when and where it stopped.

After a short time, the signal stopped moving and they were able to get an address where it had stopped. The vet's receptionist soon let my parents know where the signal had stopped. Both my parents got into their car and rushed to the address that the vet had given them.

My white-haired parent knocked on the door and spoke to the man that lived there. He explained to him that his cat was lost. "Her name is Minx, and she has a tracker in her collar that we tracked to this address.

Do you know anything about my cat?" he asked. The man explained he had just bought a new cat from a breeder and invited him in to see it.

As my white-haired parent approached the cage, he was disappointed that it wasn't Minx. It was a ginger male cat with a black stripe down its back, and black tips on his ears, and Minx was a white furry female cat. He had a tear in his eye and couldn't understand why the tracker had brought him to this address. Spanner had recognised the white-haired human! He was Minx's parent, and he was so relieved and excited to see him, thinking that he would take him home to his parents. But the white-haired person never recognised him because of the black stripe on his back and black-tipped ears. However, he did notice the cat in the cage had a tartan collar and asked if he could see it as it looked like Minx's.

His owner told him the collar had been on Spanner when they picked him up. He took the collar off and handed it to my white-haired parent.

They both examined it, and on the inside of the collar, written in pen, was 'MINX' and Minx's address. It *was* my collar!

He asked if he could keep the collar, and could he give him the address of the dealer who had sold him this cat? He agreed, and they left with the collar and the address. Poor Spanner looked so sad and was left behind, crying. Both parents quickly jumped back into their car and set off to the address of the dealer.

Chapter Six

Meanwhile... back at the farmhouse.

The two men were arguing about money. The man with the limp was in a bad mood. He hauled me off the table and I bounced about inside the cage, banging off all the sides. He took me back to the barn, opened the barn door, and just threw the cage into the barn. It crashed into the other cages and fell to the ground. He slammed the barn door shut.

My head had crashed off the side of the cage as it hit the other cages and I passed out. I don't know how long for, but when I woke my eyes would not focus.

Through blurred vision I could see four eyes staring at me, and as my eyes focused, I realised my cage had burst open when it had been thrown and struck the other cages and hit the ground. The cage door was open, and I was lying next to it.

The light was shining in my eyes from a crack in the wooden door. The four eyes were still looking at me, but I couldn't make out what or who it was because the eyes were too close.

As I pulled myself back into focus, I could see two dogs hanging over me, staring at me and drooling all over me. Dogs don't like cats, and I found myself fighting them off. They got the better of me and I passed out again.

Chapter Seven

Meanwhile… back with my parents.

My parents were travelling to the address they had been given. They were driving down a long and winding country road, and as they approached the farmhouse, they could see a man with a limp coming out of the barn. They recognised him as their pet food delivery driver. His delivery van with the cat and dog stickers on it was parked there too. They parked their car out of sight and walked towards the farmhouse.

The man with the limp hadn't noticed them and had returned into his house. My parents could hear noises, dogs barking and snarling, as if they were fighting. The noise was coming from the barn. They changed directions and walked towards the barn where I was. As they approached the barn, they could see a crack in the barn door. My white-haired parent bent down, looking through the crack in the door.

He could hear the dogs fighting and snarling but couldn't see anything. A man's voice shouted, "STOP!"

The man with the limp had seen them and was right behind my white-haired parent when he shouted, "STOP." They both got a fright. "What are you doing here? This is private property," said the man. He never recognised them and tried to direct them away from the barn. My white-haired parent stopped and explained why he was there.

He told him about the collar and where he'd got it. The man with the limp looked very shady and guilty. He said he knew nothing about his cat or the collar and to get off his land. My parents asked about the dogs barking in the barn, and if there were any cats in there.

He shouted, "NO!" and, "Get off my land. NOW!"

They had no choice but to make their way back to the car. My parents had a feeling I was in the barn. They planned to wait till it was dark and return. They hid in a lane nearby the farmhouse.

Chapter Eight

It was a very, very cold night. They sat in the car for about an hour waiting for darkness. Then they made their way back up the lane with the car lights off and parked the car near to the barn.

My white-haired parent took a torch from his car and walked to the barn, being careful no one saw him. When he got to the barn door it was locked. He shone his torch through the crack in the door. A couple of large dogs jumped at the door making him fall back onto the ground.

The dogs were barking and snarling through the crack in the door.

He heard someone come out the farmhouse and slam the door. They probably heard the dogs barking and wanted to see if everything was okay. He saw a torchlight waving and coming towards him. He quickly ran round the side of the barn and hid behind some farmyard machinery.

The man with the limp had reached the barn door. He pulled on the padlock and chain. It was still locked, so he went to the corner of the barn and shone his light close to where my white-haired parent stood, not noticing him as he hid behind the farm machinery.

He went back to the barn door. It was all quiet as he put his key into the lock and turned it. As he tried to open it, the door jammed. He pulled hard on it and it opened with a bang. The two large dogs lunged at him, knocking him back flat onto the ground. The dogs ran over him and ran off into the darkness.

When he fell, his torch flew up in the air and landed on the ground next to my white-haired parent and the light shone directly at him. He stood very still as he watched the man with the limp get to his feet. The man with the limp was growling mad and walked towards my white-haired parent, picking up his torch on the way. My white-haired parent stood very still. He still hadn't noticed him. Then he went off to look for the missing dogs.

My white-haired parent watched him as his torchlight got smaller and smaller as he walked further into the distance. My white-haired parent came out from behind the farm machinery. The barn door was open; he turned his torch back on and went inside. He shone his torch deep inside the dark barn. He saw many piercing eyes reflected at him.

There were rows of cats and dogs stacked up high in cages. He slowly crept along the rows of cages shining his torch into every cage, lighting each one up. They all looked incredibly sad and scared. He worked his way along the row, hoping that Minx would be there, somewhere. Sadly, she wasn't, so he decided to look one more time.

As he did, he noticed a black and white cat just lying in a corner of the barn and it wasn't moving like the others.

As he got closer, he shone the light right onto the cat. He could see no movement. It had some marks on it as if it had been in a fight. It was a white cat, but not Minx. This one had a black stripe down its back and black-tipped ears.

He sat down next to the cat and picked the cat up to see if he could help it.

The cat was very cold, its legs dropped over his arms like a rag doll would. He sat down and held her in close, trying to heat the cat up and comfort it. He tried rubbing her back to revive her. He noticed something on her fur, and when he looked closely, it looked like oil. He shone his torch directly onto the cat's face and wiped the oil from its ears. His eyes lit up as he realised it was MINX – it was me!

My oil-stained fur had changed me so much. I began to respond as my white-haired parent warmed me up. My eyes opened. I was so glad to see him. We could hear dogs barking outside, and he quickly got to his feet. He rushed outside carrying me. He could see a torchlight in the distance and hear the dogs barking, coming towards the barn. He turned his torch off and made his way back to the car.

We heard the man with the limp shouting. He was getting closer and closer to us. The dogs were barking and snarling and straining on their outstretched leads, almost pulling the man with the limp off his feet. I was scared.

My white-haired parent started running, and shouted, "START THE CAR." My blonde-haired parent heard him. She tried, I heard the engine trying to start, but didn't.

Chapter Nine

The man with the limp got closer. The dogs got louder as they got closer; they were nearly on us.

We just managed to get into the car and slammed the door shut; we just made it.

The dogs' paws were up on the window, scratching frantically. We could see their claws and teeth snarling, their breath and saliva steaming up the windows of the car, barking at us.

The car suddenly started up; its wheels spun in the loose gravel, kicking up dirt and mud all over the dogs and the man with the limp. I looked out the back window as we sped away.

The man with the limp was raging and shaking his fist; his face was scarlet with anger.

My parents got me home and called the police, explaining everything. They got me bathed and dried. I was looking good again. They were *soo* glad to have me back, and the right colour. I was *soo* glad to be back too. But all I could think about was Spanner.

Did he get back home? Would I ever see him again?

It was an awfully long night. I fell asleep but couldn't wait till morning. It was early when I got up and ran immediately to my cat flap. As I jumped towards it to get out, I realised I didn't have my collar on. But it was too late: I crashed into the cat flap and landed in a heap on the floor below it. Dazed, I got up and searched to find another way out. I needed to see if Spanner was okay. I ran to the front window and jumped up onto the windowsill.

HORROR, there was the pet food supply van at the bottom of the driveway! It had the same cat, dog, and chicken stickers on it as the one we were locked up in. I screamed as I ran to the back door. I could see the man with the limp's shadow bending down at the cat flap, his dogs barking and snarling trying to get in. I couldn't move. He seemed to disappear for a moment – I was *soo* scared. *BANG!* The cat flap shot open. I still couldn't believe it; it was like a bad dream. The man with the limp had my tartan collar on his neck; that's how the cat flap opened.

His head was sticking through the cat flap, shouting, "COME HERE, MINX." He was wearing a bright red bandana and his left eye was bloodshot. He got through the cat flap – it looked impossible. The two dogs got through too; he was breathing fire from his mouth every time he called out my name, "MINX." Fires shot out all around me. He was on his knees crawling towards me. The dogs were snarling behind him. I walked backwards into a corner as they got closer to me. The dogs were still barking and snarling behind him, and as they got closer the dogs got louder and louder. I screamed, and screamed, and screamed. Until my blonde-haired parent shook me, and woke me up: I had been dreaming in my bed. I was *soo* relieved – no fires, no man with a limp, no snarling. Awe, but sadly no Spanner too.

Just then my blonde-haired parent picked me up and cuddled me, carefully taking me to the front door, putting me down on the door step, and said, "Spanner's waiting." I looked up at her, paused for a second, then ran out of the house and towards Spanner's house, jumping up and onto his windowsill to see if I could see him, but no, he wasn't there. I jumped down and ran round to the back of his house. I looked through his back door. I couldn't see him or his parents; I was so sad, thinking I'd lost him.

My head was down as I walked around the side of his house and sat where I normally sat. I waited for a while, hoping he would appear. I walked back towards my house, and just as I got there, a car turned the corner. It was Spanner's parents' old car. It zoomed past me then stopped suddenly; his parents got out. I rushed back towards them. His parents were out of the car, and when they saw me, they crouched down to stroke me. My eyes were looking everywhere to see if Spanner was there. Then suddenly his face appeared in a window of the car. When our eyes met it was special.

Now I don't know if cats can smile, but I'm sure he did, and so did I. His parents opened the door.

I was so glad to see him as he rushed over to me; our fur brushed together. I think that might have been a cuddle.

We had a great afternoon together that day, the best.

It was good to be back home.

CHEE… (I think this means 'goodbye' in your language.)

About the author

Dougie Max is married and has three sons and three grandchildren. He started writing stories three years ago after telling them aloud sparked a desire to see them in print.

Matador